TURTLE HAS 3 LEGS

ISBN 10: 1-933817-70-4
ISBN 13: 978-1-933817-70-5

Published by: Profits Publishing   http://profitspublishing.com

Canadian Address
1265 Charter Hill Drive, Coquitlam, BC, V3E 1P1
Phone: (604) 941-3041   Fax: (604) 944-7993

US Address
1300 Boblett Street, Unit A-218, Blaine, WA 98230
Phone: (866) 492-6623   Fax: (250) 493-6603

SPECIAL DEDICATION

Thank you to elementary school teachers who diligently embed not only knowledge but acceptance; teaching our children that although some of us may be different we are all special.

Written by Paula J Kolins

At a beautiful lake, not so far away, there lived a friendly turtle.

Turtle was a very nice turtle.

He was also very special - he only had three legs.

Even though he could do most things, other animals at the lake thought turtle was strange because he only had three legs.

They did not want to play with him, so Turtle moved to the other side of the lake.

Turtle loved his new home. The sun kept him nice and warm. The water kept him nice and cool. The trees and bushes made a comfy place to sleep.

Yes, Turtle loved his new home. But there was one thing missing… friends!

Turtle was very lonely. If only he had some friends to play with.

That would make his new home perfect.

One day while Turtle was sunning himself on the rocks at the edge of the lake, a beautiful swan came by.

Turtle asked the beautiful swan to be his friend.

When the beautiful swan saw Turtle only had three legs, she laughed and said,

"Oh, no! I could not possibly be your friend. I am a beautiful swan and you are just a turtle and a three-legged turtle at that!"

Turtle explained to Swan that even though he only had three legs, he was very nice and would be a very good friend.

Swan thought about what Turtle said and decided she could always do with another friend.

Turtle and Swan became very good friends.

1   2   3   4

A few days later, while Turtle was taking a swim near the edge of the lake, a beaver swam by.

The beaver was very busy making a dam.

Turtle asked if he might help. When the beaver saw Turtle only had three legs, he laughed and said, "Oh, no! You could not possibly help me. Making a dam is very hard work and requires a lot of swimming. I am a busy beaver and you are just a turtle - and a three-legged turtle at that!"

Turtle explained to Beaver that even though he only had three legs, he was an excellent swimmer, and with his help the dam would be finished more quickly.

Beaver thought about what Turtle said and decided to let him help. The dam was quickly finished and Turtle and Beaver became very good friends.

One breezy summer afternoon, while Turtle, Swan and Beaver were taking a walk in a nearby field, a bunny hopped by.

The three friends invited Bunny to join them. When Bunny saw Turtle only had three legs, he laughed and said, "Oh, no! I could not possibly walk with you. I am a very fast bunny and you are just a turtle - and a three-legged turtle at that! You would only slow me down."

"That is fine," Swan and Beaver said, angrily. "You go off by yourself. We will stay with our friend, Turtle!" Bunny hopped away as fast as a rocket.

Turtle turned to his friends and said, "Thank you for being the best friends I could ever ask for!"

From that day on, Turtle was never lonely again.

He even forgot he only had three legs.

The End

Interesting Learning Facts

Turtles

- There are over 300 different types of turtles
- Some types of turtles can live over 100 years
- Turtles have lived on Earth for more than 200 million years
- The shell of a turtle has 60 different bones connected together
- Turtles protect themselves by pulling their bodies inside their shells
- Turtles have excellent eyesight as well as sense of smell
- Baby turtles are called hatchlings

1 2 3 4 5 6 7 8 9

BEAVERS

SWANS

- Swans are one of the largest flying birds in the world

- The average swan weighs 15 to 25 pounds

- Beavers are strong and intelligent animals

- Swans live up to 25 years in the wild and up to 50 years in captivity

- Beavers are very hard workers and use their teeth to cut and chew wood

- Swans have over 25,000 feathers

- Beavers' front teeth never stop growing

- Beavers live for about 16 years

- Swans have the longest neck of any bird,with 23 to 25 vertebrae

- Beavers can swim 5 miles per hour

- Beavers can stay under water for over 15 minutes

- Swans eat tiny fish and tadpoles, as well as other aquatic vegetation

- A beaver's fur is oily and waterproof

- Swans will remember you if you have been kind to them

- Beavers eat bark, roots, leaves and twigs

- Baby beavers are called kits

- Baby swans are called cygnets

LaVergne, TN USA
09 February 2011
215814LV00004B

ISBN 978-1-933817-70-5

90000

9 781933 817705